How do plants grow?

T0327773

Written by Susannah Reed

Illustrated by Victor Tavares

Collins

What's in this book?

Listen and say

flowers

beans

nuts

lemon

apple

pear

mango

banana

cherries

Download the audio at www.collins.co.uk/839663

🎧 Emi and Ko are at their grandma's house. They're eating cherries.

"*Mmm.* I love cherries," said Emi.

"Me, too," said Ko. "Where do cherries come from, Grandma?"

"Cherries come from plants," said Grandma. "They grow on trees. A small cherry grows into a big cherry tree."

"But how?" asked Ko. "How do plants grow?"

There are lots of plants.
Flowers, vegetables and grass are all
plants. Trees are big plants. Most plants
have leaves and grow in the ground.

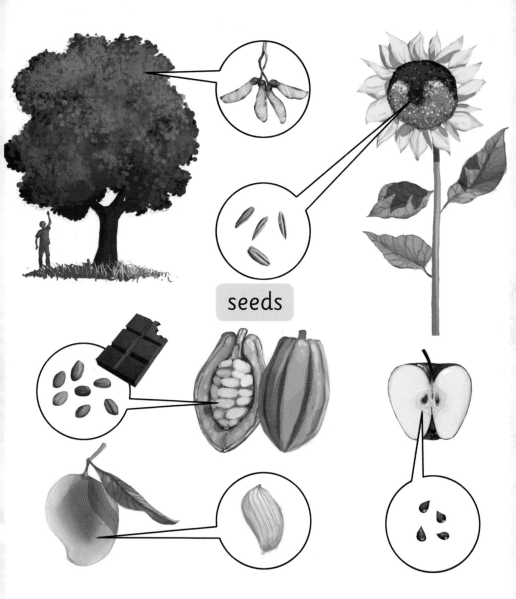

seeds

Plants have seeds. Some seeds come from flowers. Some come from trees and fruit. Seeds can be big or small.

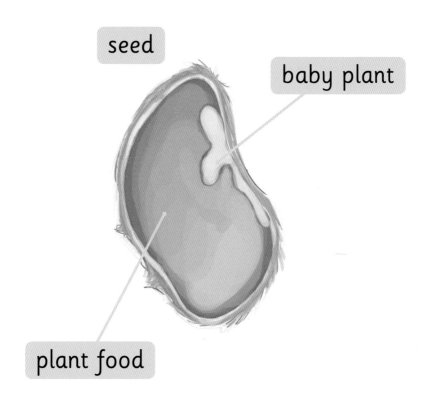

seed

baby plant

plant food

In a seed there is a very small baby plant.
And there is some food for the baby plant.

How does the baby plant in a seed grow?
First, we plant the seed in the ground.

The baby plant needs food, water and sun.
It has food in the seed. We give the plant
lots of water.

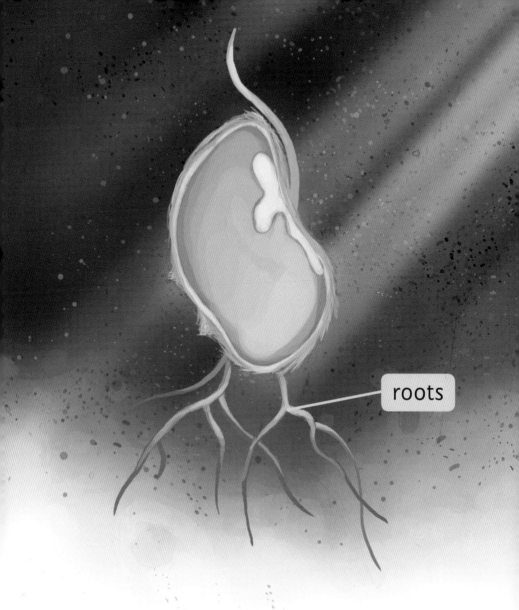

roots

The sun is hot today. The baby plant
grows up to the sun. The roots of the plant
grow down into the ground.

Now the plant is bigger and it has leaves.
The leaves and the sun make more food
for the plant.

water   food

Food and water move between the leaves and the roots. They move up and down the plant.

The plant gets bigger and bigger.
Some plants grow flowers. Some plants
grow vegetables or fruit.

Can you see the beans and bananas on
these plants?

Some seeds grow into trees. Some trees grow nuts.

Some trees grow fruit. These trees grow cherries, apples, pears, mangoes, lemons and oranges.

Can you see the fruit on each tree?
Which do you like eating?

Fruit and nut trees grow flowers in the spring. This is a cherry tree. Can you see the flowers? They are cherry blossom.

Cherry blossom flowers are pink or white.

In the summer, the blossom falls to the ground and big red cherries grow on the tree.

Cherries have seeds in them.

The cherries fall from the tree and
the seeds move into the ground.
Then new cherry trees can grow!

20

"I love cherries!" said Emi.

"Me, too," said Ko. "Let's eat them, and plant the seeds."

"Good idea," said Emi.

Picture dictionary

Listen and repeat

blossom

leaf

plant

plant a seed

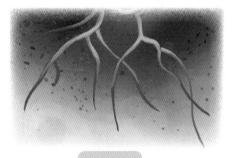

root

spring

summer